# TRICK OR Treat!

ON/OFF

On every page, shine your light to see what's hiding in the night!

For **Jasper** and **Molly** – two adorable, little monsters!

make believe ideas

Michael has the HEEBIE-JEEBIES —
the WORST you've ever seen.
And there's one SCARY reason why:
Today is

# HALLOWEEN!

It's time to TRICK-or-TREAT in town —

EXCITEMENT'S in the air.

His sister, Meg, is THRILLED to bits;

she loves a little SCARE!

Meg YELLS,
"Let's brave the DEEP, DARK NIGHT

in search of something SWEET!"
She SKIPS up to a
SPOOKY house . . .

and SHOUTS out,
"TRICK
or
TREAT!"

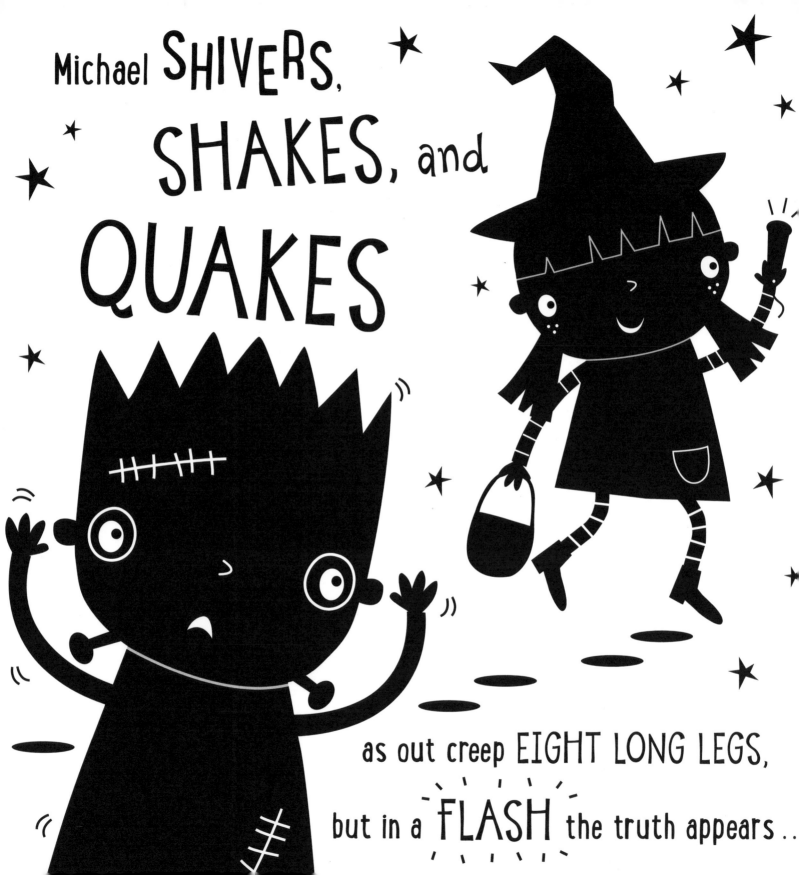

Michael SHIVERS, SHAKES, and QUAKES

as out creep EIGHT LONG LEGS,
but in a FLASH the truth appears . . .

"It's just a BOY!" says Meg.

The next door opens with a

# BOOOOO

when Meg CALLS,

## "TRICK
## or
## TREAT!"

While Michael WHIMPERS

Meg reVEALS . . .

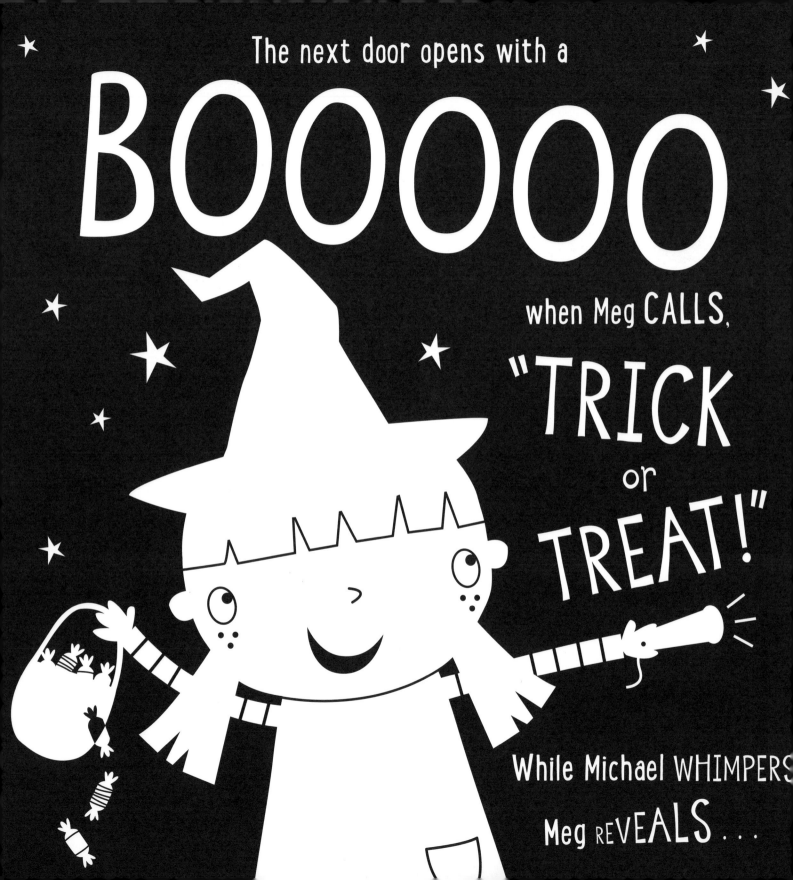

a LADY in a SHEET!

They TRICK-OR-TREAT
along the road –
a MONSTER
at each door.

CREEAK!

Poor Michael
TREMBLES with each step.

Meg shouts,
"THERE'S JUST
ONE MORE ..."

The **FINAL HOUSE** sits on a hill,
its **GIANT** gates shut tight,
with **WARNING** signs
that say...

KEEP OUT,

JUST SCRAM,

and

DOG WILL BITE!

"They don't fool me!" Meg boldly cries.
"There's still FUN to be had!"
While Michael whispers to himself,
"I think poor Meg's gone MAD!"

The door swings open at their KNOCK;
out streams a BLAZING LIGHT.
From DEEP within, there comes a

# SCREAM

that ECHOES through the night!

"It's just a group of SKELETONS!"

Meg JUMPS around with JOY.

The SKITTISH skeletons CRY OUT,
"OH, NO!
A GIRL
AND
BOY!"

But little **Michael** has a **PLAN** —
he knows just what to do!
He **GRABS** Meg's light
and with a
**FLASH**
says, "Look,
we're just like you!"

The skeletons GASP; it's clear to see
they didn't need to FUSS.
"They're just TWO little bags of BONES —
SKELETONS
just like us!"

The KIDS head HOME and wave GOOD-BYE as the TRICK-or-TREATING ends.

Meg says, "You're BRAVER than you think! And, LOOK, you've made NEW FRIENDS."

TUCKED UP in bed, the children DREAM of MONSTERS BIG and SMALL.

Now that Michael KNOWS what's UNDERNEATH, he'll make FRIENDS with them all!